"THE WINNER AIN'T THE ONE WITH THE FASTEST CAR; IT'S THE ONE WHO REFUSES TO LOSE."

DALE EARNHARDT SR.

1951–2001

An Imprint of Abdo Publishing | abdobooks.com

Lives Cut Short

Dale Earnhardt Sr.

NASCAR Legend

By Marcia Amidon Lusted

CREDITS

abdobooks.com

Published by Abdo Publishing, a division of ABDO, PO Box 398166, Minneapolis, Minnesota 55439.

Printed in the United States of America, North Mankato, Minnesota.
082020
092020

Cover Photo: John Cordes/Icon Sportswire/Getty Images
Interior Photos: John Cordes/Icon Sportswire/Getty Images, 1; Warren Wimmer/AP Images, 7, 62; Action Sports Photography/Shutterstock Images, 9; Roger Simms/Daytona Beach News Journal/AP Images, 13; Dozier Mobley/Getty Images Sport Classic/Getty Images, 14, 35, 47, 53, 97 (top), 99 (top); Gary O'Brien/The Charlotte Observer/AP Images, 17; Epix Productions/Shutterstock Images, 20; RacingOne/ISC Archives/Getty Images, 22, 31, 42, 45, 61, 97 (bottom); AP Images, 25; Grindstone Media Group/Shutterstock Images, 28, 32, 40–41, 51, 57, 59, 83, 87, 96; iStockphoto, 38; Bruce Alan Bennett/Shutterstock Images, 49, 85; Bruce Ackerman/AP Images, 55, 98; James R. Martin/Shutterstock Images, 67; Amy Conn/AP Images, 71; Phelan Ebenhack/Orlando Sentinel/AP Images, 73; Tami Chappell/Reuters/Newscom, 77; Sam Morris/STR/Reuters/Newscom, 78; Chuck Burton/AP Images, 90, 99 (bottom); Malachi Jacobs/Shutterstock Images, 93, 94

Editor: Alyssa Krekelberg
Series Designer: Becky Daum

Library of Congress Control Number: 2020932977
Publisher's Cataloging-in-Publication Data
Names: Lusted, Marcia Amidon, author.
Title: Dale Earnhardt Sr.: NASCAR legend / by Marcia Amidon Lusted
Other title: NASCAR legend
Description: Minneapolis, Minnesota : Abdo Publishing, 2021 | Series: Lives cut short | Includes online resources and index
Identifiers: ISBN 9781532193972 (lib. bdg.) | ISBN 9781098212780 (ebook)
Subjects: LCSH: Earnhardt, Dale (Ralph Earnhardt), 1951-2001--Juvenile literature. | Stock car drivers--United States--Biography--Juvenile literature. | Automobiles, Racing--Juvenile literature. | Motorsports--Juvenile literature. | Stock car racing--Accidents--Juvenile literature.
Classification: DDC 796.72092--dc23

Table of Contents

1

The Race of a Lifetime

It was the morning of February 15, 1998, in Daytona Beach, Florida. The Daytona 500, NASCAR's signature race, would start in just a few hours. The season-opening event is a 500-mile (805 km) race for professional stock car drivers. That day, Richard Childress arrived at the track. He was the owner of the Richard Childress Racing team, and he was worried about his No. 3 Chevrolet race car, which would be driven by Dale Earnhardt Sr. Too many things had gone wrong with the car in previous races.

▸ Dale Earnhardt Sr. was one of the most well-known NASCAR drivers.

Childress was hoping for a win, but every time Earnhardt had competed in the Daytona 500, something had happened to keep him from the top position. Various mishaps always seemed to hold Earnhardt back, such as hitting a seagull on the track, running out of gas, and cutting a tire on a piece of metal. He had finished second in 1984, 1993, 1995, and 1996. He finished third in 1989. Now, in a streak that began in March 1996, Earnhardt hadn't won in 59 straight races.

Earnhardt spent a long time checking his race car that morning. He wanted to make sure everything was perfect and that the newly installed engine was running correctly. Then he got ready to run the race. Childress later commented that he had never seen Earnhardt acting so upbeat and optimistic before a race. When driver Jeff Gordon, who was the defending Daytona 500 champion, asked Earnhardt, "Are you going to win your first Daytona 500 today?"[1]

NASCAR's Beginnings

The National Association for Stock Car Auto Racing (NASCAR) is the organization that governs and operates stock car racing. It was founded in 1948 and remains a popular racing organization today. Bill France Sr., an auto mechanic who dabbled in racing, helped found NASCAR. France was known for organizing races and wanted to establish a string of events that would lead to one national stock car champion. He worked with race car drivers and owners to build the racing series that would become NASCAR.

▲ Cars can reach speeds of about 200 miles per hour (320 kmh) on the Daytona track.

Earnhardt just lowered his sunglasses and stared at Gordon in a way that seemed to say that if Gordon got in his way, he'd better watch out.

Vying for Position

Starting positions for the Daytona 500 are based on the fastest times in an earlier series of qualifying races. When the race began, Earnhardt was fourth out of a total of 43 cars.

Drivers must complete 200 laps around the 2.5-mile (4 km) racetrack. The entire time, they're vying for that first-place position. On Lap 17, Earnhardt made his move. One car stood between him and a clear racetrack. Earnhardt twisted his steering wheel to the right, accelerated, and then pulled in front of the field—taking the lead for the first time.

The Daytona International Speedway has a reputation for crashes. This race, however, didn't have the usual number of crashes and other mishaps. It also didn't have many yellow caution flags, which require all drivers to slow down and line up behind the pace car. Earnhardt's strengths as a driver were especially suited to races where there were long stretches of laps under a green flag, meaning drivers can drive as fast as possible with no cautions to slow them down.

On Lap 140, Earnhardt took the lead for the fifth time in the race. A few laps later, the cars driven by Robert Pressley and John Andretti crashed, resulting in a caution flag that slowed the other racers. The racing flag went back to green with just over 57 miles (92 km) remaining in the race. A voice suddenly spoke from the radio in Earnhardt's car: "Hey, Sunday Money, this is

Captain Jack. Why don't you go out there and snag that big one today?"[2]

The mysterious Captain Jack was Bill France Jr. He was the son of NASCAR's founder. It was unusual for someone like France to speak to a driver during a race, especially to urge him to try harder and win. But it seemed to work.

A crash on the track forced the drivers to race under a caution flag from Lap 174 to 177. The race restarted on Lap 178, and Earnhardt was still in the lead position. But he and his crew were nervous. Earnhardt had been in this position many times before, leading with just a few laps to go, and yet still lost the race. There was another crash on Lap 199, and another caution flag was thrown out. Earnhardt was

Racing Flags

NASCAR and other types of auto racing use a universal system of colored flags for communicating with drivers during a race. These flags are waved to let drivers know what's going on. The green flag signals that a race is either starting or continuing. A yellow flag means there is a hazard on the track and all drivers must slow down and line up behind the pace car. This flag is usually waved when there has been an accident or when debris is spotted on the track. A white flag means that there is only one lap left to go in the race, and a checkered flag means the race is finished. A red flag means that all competition must stop because there are dangerous conditions, such as lightning, a car on fire, or debris blocking the track. There are several other flag colors, and each has its own distinct meaning.

driving the final lap of the race under a yellow flag. According to NASCAR rules, no one is allowed to pass when there is a yellow caution flag. That meant, because he was in first place, no other driver could pass Earnhardt. He crossed the finish line and the checkered flag was waved. He was the winner of the 1998 Daytona 500. After so many tries, he had finally won.

A Lucky Penny

On the morning of the 1998 Daytona 500, a young girl named Wessa Miller and her parents drove 750 miles (1,200 km) to meet Earnhardt.[3] Wessa suffered from spina bifida, a disease that meant she had to use a wheelchair. Wessa loved racing, and through the Make-A-Wish Foundation she got the chance to meet Earnhardt. When she was finally face-to-face with him, Wessa gave Earnhardt a lucky penny she'd brought with her. Earnhardt immediately glued it to the dashboard of his black No. 3 Chevy, and he went on to win the race that day. When the car was later brought to the Daytona 500 museum, the penny was still there.

"A Feeling You Can't Replace"

The Childress Racing pit crew exploded with excitement. They jumped up and down and hugged one another—their driver had done it! Earnhardt pulled off the track and made his way to Victory Lane, where the winner of a race celebrates his victory. Pit crews from every team lined up to greet him. He drove slowly, giving high fives to anyone who wanted them.

Earnhardt then radioed France and asked, "Captain Jack, is it OK if I do a

▲ Earnhardt was congratulated by the pit crews before he could step out of his car.

burnout on your grass?" France replied, "It's all yours, pal."[4] The Daytona winner pulled his car onto the perfectly kept green grass decorating the racetrack. Earnhardt then whipped his car in circles, leaving dark tire marks behind in celebration of his victory.

Earnhardt later recalled the moment when he won the 1998 Daytona 500—the race that he had been chasing for so long. "It's a feeling you can't replace," he said. "It's eluded us for so many

▲ Earnhardt throws his fists up in celebration after winning his first Daytona 500.

years. . . . I never believed, when guys told me how good it felt to win the 500. I never believed it, but I do now. It sure feels good."[5]

Earnhardt was known for approaching each race with determination, guts, and perseverance. Throughout his career he earned several nicknames, including the Man in Black because of his black No. 3 Chevrolet race car, and the Intimidator because of how he raced. Although the NASCAR star's life came to an untimely end in 2001, at the same track where he celebrated his Daytona 500 win, his legacy would live on.

2

A Legacy of Racing

Ralph Dale Earnhardt Sr. was born on April 29, 1951, in Kannapolis, North Carolina. Kannapolis was a mill town with a population of fewer than 30,000 people at that time.[1] Many people there worked at Cannon Mills, which was a textile mill that made towels, sheets, and other fabrics.

Dale was the third child of Martha and Ralph Earnhardt. Ralph worked for Cannon Mills, and Martha was a waitress in a diner. Dale would eventually have four siblings: brothers Danny and

▸ Many workers in Kannapolis, North Carolina, relied on the mill for steady income.

FIELDCREST
NON
STOP

Randy and sisters Kathy and Kaye. When he was born, Dale's parents lived in a neighborhood of Kannapolis that was called Car Town, so called because the streets were named after car brands and types popular at the time. They included names such as Buick, Cadillac, Ford, and Coach. The Earnhardt house was on Sedan Avenue.

In addition to working at the mill, Dale's father had a second job. Ralph helped out by working on cars in a garage, and the owner there had a race car that he drove in local dirt track races. The Kannapolis area was surrounded by many small dirt tracks, and racing was the number one sport in the area. One day the

Dirt Track Racing

Dirt track racing is a kind of auto racing that takes place on an oval track. However, the track is made of dirt or clay instead of pavement. Often, fairgrounds have dirt horse racing tracks, so it is easy to use these for automobile races as well. Dirt track racing is still popular, and there are more than 1,500 dirt tracks in the United States. Dirt tracks are almost always one mile (1.6 km) or less in length, and clay is the preferred surface because it is less dusty and cars can stick to it better.[2]

Dirt track racing resulted in the development of two different types of cars: stock cars and open-wheel cars. Open-wheel cars are lighter and more responsive, but they can be fragile, and drivers cannot bump each other. Stock cars tend to be heavier and a little slower, but drivers can bump and nudge other cars without worrying about breaking them. They are also better for endurance races.

owner was sick and couldn't race, so Ralph drove instead. Soon, Ralph was hooked on dirt track racing. He quit his mill job and began racing full time. He was both a driver and a mechanic.

Ralph was different from many of the other dirt track racers. Other people only raced on weekends and otherwise had day jobs. Ralph had a young family and not much money, so he had to be careful with his car. He couldn't afford to wreck his vehicle. Despite his reluctance to drive aggressively and make risky moves, Ralph was one of the best dirt track racers in North Carolina. He won a NASCAR Sportsman Championship in 1956.

The Ford Fix

During one dirt track racing season in the mid-1950s, all the drivers of certain Ford cars were facing the same problem: a small part on their cars called the axle key kept breaking. The axle key was a square metal rod with a tapered end. It was the part of the axle that the car's wheels locked onto. This key kept breaking because it had not been made strong enough for racing use. However, Ralph had a secret. He had taken a regular screwdriver manufactured by Sears and cut off the top and the end to make a better, stronger version of the axle key. Once his secret was out, every driver rushed to the nearby Sears store to buy that same size screwdriver, only to be told that "some guy from Kannapolis" kept coming there and buying them all.[3]

THE MAN IN THE PINK CAR

As Dale grew up, he spent time with his dad in the family's garage, learning about mechanics and working on engines. Dale also fell in love

▲ Kids still enjoy racing slot cars today.

with racing. He started racing slot cars, which are miniature toy race cars that run in a slot or groove on a small racetrack. He even won a racing trophy.

Dale was happiest hanging out in his dad's garage, listening to men who came to talk about racing and engines with his father. By the time Dale was ten, he was traveling with his father to races. Once he was a teenager, he and his brothers became part of Ralph's pit crew. At age 16, Dale quit school. He had struggled with his studies and found school to be boring. He was eager to go out into the adult world. In 1968, at just 17 years old, Dale married Latane Brown, and their first son, Kerry, was born in 1969.

It wasn't until he was 19, in 1971, that Dale drove in his first real auto race, at the Concord Speedway in Concord, North Carolina. Dale was working odd jobs as a mechanic and a welder at the time, and there was little money for him to buy a race car of his own. Dale's neighbors, racers Ray and David Oliver, had recently gotten a new race car, and they gave their old one to Dale. The car was a 1956 Ford Club Sedan. It looked more like a family car than a race car.

Dale began working on the car with help from his dad. They spent hours rebuilding it,

Kerry Earnhardt and His Father

Between the ages of five and 16, Kerry Earnhardt didn't see his dad. His parents had gotten divorced when he was one year old. Eventually, Kerry and his father got reacquainted. "It was like we never left off," Kerry noted. "When we got back together, it was just like the typical relationship. We had a lot of fun together. We worked on cars together. We just had a good time with it."[4]

Kerry tried his luck in the NASCAR world in the 1990s. He earned Rookie of the Year in 1992 but never reached the fame his father had. Kerry retired in 2007.

▲ Dale, *left*, became close friends with other drivers, such as Neil Bonnett.

fine-tuning the engine, and putting new tires on the car. Dale and his friends thought that a new coat of paint might make the car seem more like a real race car. They were aiming for a green color, but something went wrong with the paint, and it came out pink. So, Dale drove his very first race in a pink car. There are no written records of that race, including who the other drivers were and how many cars participated. But according to his friends, Dale finished in tenth place.

Backward Biking

Young Dale Earnhardt loved bicycles, and he often built them himself. But Dale also developed a unique talent of being able to ride a bicycle backward just as well as he could ride one forward. He would sit backward on the bicycle and pedal, holding the handlebars behind him. As an adult racing at the Dover International Speedway in Delaware, Earnhardt once showed off his backward biking ability by pedaling around the oval horse track at the speedway.

David Oliver, who also raced that day, got an impression of what Dale was like as a racer. "You could see that Dale knew what he was doing," Oliver said. "He wasn't like someone just starting out. He knew when to make the move and when not to make the move, where the holes were. He knew things I didn't know."[5]

3

Beginning His Career

With his first real race under his belt, Earnhardt was now thoroughly hooked on dirt track racing. It was all he wanted to do. It took a toll on his family, however, and in 1970 he and his wife Latane divorced. Earnhardt did not keep up with paying child support for his son, Kerry. Earnhardt worked manual labor jobs, looking for anything that would provide him with enough money to go racing. He needed a new race car.

By 1973, Earnhardt was working in a wheel alignment shop in Concord, North Carolina.

▸ Earnhardt's aggressive driving style earned him many wins.

ton
union
Wrangler

He had gotten married to Brenda Gee a year before, and they had a daughter named Kelley. In 1974, their son Dale Jr. was born.

The family lived in various trailers and small apartments, constantly moving because they didn't have enough money for rent. Earnhardt was often behind on paying his bills. The constant money troubles put a strain on his young family. Racing costs money, and Earnhardt often took out loans for racing needs. Racing came first, even when it meant depriving his family members of what they needed, like better housing and reliable cars for everyday driving. Earnhardt later said, "Racing cost me my second marriage for the things I took away from my family."[1] His marriage to Brenda ended in 1977.

Throughout this time, Earnhardt was continually scouting for another new car that he could fix up and race. Ralph Earnhardt sent him to see James Miller, another race car owner and former

A NASCAR Family

Earnhardt's second wife, Brenda Gee, came from a NASCAR background. Her father, Robert Gee, was a well-known race car builder who put together winning cars for many NASCAR drivers. Brenda met Earnhardt when he was driving several of her father's cars, which led to their relationship. After their divorce in 1977, Brenda continued to work in the world of racing for the company JR Motorsports as an accounting specialist. She died of cancer in 2019 at the age of 65.

driver who had a junkyard behind his house. The junkyard contained several Ford Falcon cars, which Miller used to fix up and race but now had no need for. Earnhardt went to see Miller after work one day and asked him about driving one of the Falcons. Miller told him that he could drive a car if he did some work on it. They had a deal. Earnhardt fixed up a 1956 Falcon and began racing it. As Miller later recalled:

> *Dale was good but we wore out that car that first year. He crashed everywhere. He was just trying things, seeing what he could do. He'd see a hole [between cars on the track] and think he could make it through, and sometimes he could but sometimes he couldn't. Ralph would talk with him, teach him what to do.*[2]

Earnhardt was learning how to race. In 1973, Miller built a new garage at his house, and he and Earnhardt began fixing up another Falcon. Ralph spent a great deal of time there, working on the car with his son and Miller. Ralph was at the Concord Speedway when Dale won his first race in the Falcon. It was the first of several races he won that year.

▲ Racing is a serious business. Crashes can happen even with talented veteran drivers at the wheel.

From Dirt to Asphalt

On September 26, 1973, Ralph died of a heart attack at age 45. Earnhardt was left to navigate the racing world alone. "Daddy had begun to help me with engine work and give me used tires, and he'd talked to Mama about putting me in his car," Earnhardt said. "Then he died. It left me in a situation where I had to make it on my own."[3]

Earnhardt transitioned from racing on dirt tracks to racing on asphalt tracks. Asphalt racing paid more money in prizes than dirt track racing did. Earnhardt bought another used race car, fixed it up, and then started driving in the NASCAR Late Model Sportsman Circuit. This was his entry into professional racing.

The NASCAR Late Model Sportsman Circuit started out as a disorganized series of regional races that took place

Dale on His Dad

In a 1986 interview with the *Charlotte Observer*, Earnhardt talked about his father:

Daddy was honest, quiet, and independent. I think it was his independence that maybe was the reason he didn't go much further in racing. Lord knows he had the know-how to go on. I stood on his tow truck as a boy, and I think I must have seen every lap he ever drove. I guess you would say I adopted his style of driving and I try to capitalize on what he told me, all the advice he gave me. I wish I'd paid more attention. It has been a long time, but he's still an everyday thought. Whenever I have a problem, inside the race car or out, I still think, "How would he have handled this situation? What would he have done?" He's still a big part of me.[4]

before a big NASCAR Cup Series race. The name of the series has changed over the years, as have the cars. In 1974, the races were still small, and the cars were not high tech.

The Late Model Sportsman division races took place in several different places, and drivers had just one car, which they towed to races with a pickup truck. There was no backup car or extra crews or equipment. Some drivers made enough money racing on the Sportsman Circuit that they could focus only on that one series, instead of having to split their time between different racing circuits. The series also allowed racers to keep their regular jobs, which was very important to Earnhardt with a growing family to support.

Although Earnhardt had very little money and had to use a race car meant for

NASCAR Racing Series

In 2020, NASCAR had four major racing series: the Cup Series, the Xfinity Series, the Gander RV & Outdoors Truck Series, and the ARCA Menards Series. Many of the names have changed over the years, usually depending on the company that is sponsoring the series. The Cup Series is the top circuit. It has production stock cars that are similar in appearance, but they are branded with the car company of the model they are based on, such as Ford or Chevrolet. The Xfinity Series also runs stock cars but is considered to be a series where drivers can prove themselves and move up into Cup racing. The truck series is the only racing series for modified pickup trucks. The ARCA Menards Series is a division of the Automobile Racing Club of America (ARCA) and is a semiprofessional, minor racing series where drivers can move up into bigger NASCAR series.

▲ Racing cars in the 1970s weren't as safe as racing cars today.

▲ NASCAR FANS CAN SPAN GENERATIONS.

short dirt tracks, he did well because he was a good driver. He won his first Sportsman race on July 19, 1974, at Metrolina Speedway in Charlotte, North Carolina. And soon he would continue to move up the racing ladder to the Winston Cup, which was NASCAR's top racing series.

Racing and the Oil Crisis

In late 1973, the Organization of the Petroleum Exporting Countries (OPEC) announced an embargo of oil shipments to Europe, Japan, and the United States in order to drive up the price of oil. The United States was heavily dependent on OPEC for oil and gasoline supplies. The auto racing industry was very concerned, wondering what would happen to the sport with gasoline so scarce.

In November 1973, large racing organizations, including NASCAR, met to decide what to do. At the same time the government started monitoring gas consumption. A racing committee discovered that auto racing ranked a low seventh in fuel consumption, behind other leisure activities such as vacation travel. Being this far down on the list made it less likely that all auto racing would be suspended.

The government asked all major leisure activity groups to reduce their gas use by 25 percent.[5] Auto racing took steps such as eliminating long-distance endurance races and cutting back on racing schedules. In March 1974, the OPEC oil embargo was lifted, but it took time for racing to return to normal.

4

Rising Star of NASCAR

It was Memorial Day in 1975 at the Charlotte Motor Speedway. The Charlotte 600 was underway. Earnhardt was driving in that race—his first in the Winston Cup. He was in a car owned by Ed Negre, another driver. Negre had a newer, better car to run in the race himself, so his son Norman convinced him to let Earnhardt drive the older car. Norman would be Earnhardt's crew chief—the person responsible for building the car and adjusting it for different race conditions. Negre insisted on seeing

▸ Earnhardt took off in his No. 8 car at the 1975 Charlotte 600.

08
Hinson
Const.
Co
HOTROD

Earnhardt drive before giving his permission, and after watching him race at the Metrolina Speedway, he agreed with his son that Earnhardt could drive well. Earnhardt drove the No. 8 Ed Negre Dodge Charger in the race and finished twenty-second out of 40 cars. Negre finished in thirty-second place.

Earnhardt competed in hundreds of Winston Cup races during his career, racing for several different teams. In 1978, he got his big break when he replaced another driver for the World 600 Cup at the Charlotte Motor Speedway. In the Firecracker 400 race there, Earnhardt placed seventh. More importantly, he attracted the attention of Rod Osterlund. Osterlund was an investor who owned a Winston Cup car but wasn't happy with his driver. He wanted Earnhardt on his team instead.

A Thirsty Pit Stop

The Charlotte 600 was a 600-mile (965 km) race, and Earnhardt was not used to endurance races that took a long time to complete. The weather was also very hot, and cars were equipped with a three-gallon (11 L) water jug with a straw for the driver. About one third of the way into the race, Ed Negre noticed that Earnhardt was in the pit area for an unscheduled stop. When he radioed the pit and asked why, he was told that Earnhardt had come in for a drink of water because he was thirsty. He had already finished the water jug in the car. Negre teased Earnhardt about that for the rest of his career.

RACING FOR OSTERLUND

Earnhardt began racing for Osterlund in 1978, competing in two races. His aggressive driving style had already earned him the nickname the Intimidator. In the two races he drove for Osterlund that first season, Earnhardt finished second and fourth. However, Osterlund recognized that Earnhardt was still driving as if he were racing on a dirt track—which required drivers to race crowded, often bumping each other—and that his driving style was ragged. He wanted Earnhardt to drive more smoothly, and this meant Earnhardt had to learn a more professional way of handling a race car.

The Winston Cup

NASCAR's top racing series was founded in 1949. From 1971 through 2003, it was called the Winston Cup. The sport experienced tremendous growth during this time. Television broadcasts of the races made NASCAR a household name for fans. Since 2003, the Cup Series has gone through several more sponsorship names, including Sprint, Nextel, and Monster Energy. In 2020 it was known as the NASCAR Cup Series.

The best place to receive this training was at the Bondurant School of High Performance Driving in California. The Bondurant School taught regular street motorists how to drive defensively and avoid accidents. It also taught high-performance precision driving for racers who would be driving at high speeds on

▲ It's important for race car drivers to understand how their cars work.

racetracks that were closed to other kinds of traffic. Earnhardt attended the school in 1979.

Just Go Fast

Earnhardt's relationship with Rod Osterlund Racing was a good one. He had a house to live in, which Osterlund had provided for him, and money. Earnhardt also didn't have to worry about coming up with cash for car parts and repairs. Osterlund simply wanted Earnhardt to go fast, and he did. His aggressive driving style helped him finish in the top ten of several races in California, but he was also an expensive driver for any team to maintain. "He hit just about every wall on every track we went to," Osterlund said. "What you had to know was that Dale Earnhardt was expensive. A lot of people couldn't afford him, he wrecked so many cars. . . . It cost a lot of money to keep Dale Earnhardt on the racetrack."[1]

Meeting Earnhardt

Rod Osterlund remembered his first meeting with Dale Earnhardt in 1978:

And here was this ragtag guy. That's the only way I can describe him. . . . He was divorced on the verge of bankruptcy. And he wasn't even young. He was twenty-seven years old. That's the thing a lot of people forget. Dale Earnhardt didn't start out as a young rookie. He was something else . . . he was . . . a wild young man.[2]

In the next-to-last race of the 1979 season, Osterlund replaced his permanent driver with Earnhardt. It was the 1979 Southeastern 500 at the Bristol Motor Speedway in Tennessee. The race was only the sixteenth start for Earnhardt in professional races, and he was still a new driver. Earnhardt drove Osterlund Racing's No. 2 Chevrolet car, and on Lap 474 of 500 he took the lead. He kept it until the end, beating driver Bobby Allison by three seconds to win.

However, Earnhardt's race at Pocono Raceway in Pennsylvania ended differently. As he entered turn two, called the Tunnel Turn, Earnhardt's car blew a tire, and he hit the wall. He was evacuated by helicopter and ended up with a broken

▲ THE BRISTOL MOTOR SPEEDWAY IS A CONCRETE OVAL TRACK THAT STRETCHES 0.533 MILES (0.86 KM).

collarbone, a concussion, and severe bruises. His doctor said Earnhardt nearly broke his neck.

Earnhardt missed four races, but he still managed to finish in the seventh position overall in the points standings for the Winston Cup. Earnhardt was also named the 1979 NASCAR

Rookie of the Year. Osterlund offered him a five-year contract with his racing team.

A Rookie and the Championship

In 1980, Earnhardt won five races. The Winston Cup Series champion was determined by a points system, with drivers accumulating points for

▲ Earnhardt stands proudly beside his Winston Cup trophy.

each race according to where they finished. After driving in more than 30 races all over the country, Earnhardt was just 19 points ahead of Cale Yarborough, but it was enough to earn him his first Winston Cup championship. He was only the fourth driver to have won Rookie of the Year and then quickly nail a season title. His earnings from that season totaled more than $500,000.[3]

It seemed that Earnhardt, at the age of 29, had it all in his career. He was winning big races and making good prize money, and he had a good relationship with Osterlund. But everything changed with a sudden announcement in 1981. Sixteen races into the new season, with Earnhardt defending his Winston Cup championship, Osterlund suddenly decided to quit racing.

5

THE INTIMIDATOR

The news that Rod Osterlund was done with racing came as a surprise and a shock, not only to Earnhardt but to everyone on the team. It was the middle of the racing season, and Osterlund already had a buyer for his racing team: a man named Jim Stacy.

Stacy's purchase of the Osterlund team changed everything. He bought Osterlund Racing's team for $1.7 million and promptly fired the team's racing manager, Roland Wlodyka, so he could put his own manager, Boobie

▸ EARNHARDT WASN'T THRILLED WITH THE SALE TO JIM STACY.

Dale

Harrington, in place.[1] He also fired six members of the racing crew, hired a second driver, and announced that he planned to hire more drivers until he had five racing entries.[2] Stacy would buy and sell other racing teams and would sponsor cars. Maintaining so many race cars, drivers, and teams would cost him millions of dollars each year.

Sports Image

Once Earnhardt became well known on the NASCAR circuit, fans were eager to buy souvenirs, such as T-shirts, with his name on them. To handle this demand, Earnhardt started a company in the late 1980s called Sports Image. Its purpose was to manage and distribute all Earnhardt-related souvenirs, which were sold through a network of vendors who operated trailers at every NASCAR race. These trailers sold an average of 5,000 T-shirts a day at $20 a shirt.[3] In addition, other venues away from the tracks also sold merchandise. As a result, Sports Image made $40 to $50 million every year with these souvenirs.[4] Even though Earnhardt eventually sold the company, he continued to earn royalties on every sale of his souvenir merchandise.

RICHARD CHILDRESS RACING

Earnhardt drove four races for the new owner, but he didn't like the idea of working with Stacy, a man with no previous knowledge of racing who treated the staff members as if he owned them all. Earnhardt realized that he might have other options. Just a month after Osterlund sold his team to Stacy, Earnhardt met with Richard Childress, an independent race car owner and driver. Childress was

▲ Earnhardt speaks with Childress before a 1984 race.

almost broke and struggling to keep racing. The two struck a deal.

Earnhardt would drive Childress's car for the remaining 11 races of the season. "I didn't want to get out of [driving] the car, but I knew the opportunity was there," explained Childress. "I knew Dale was a championship driver."[5]

However, Childress did not have much money, and he went into debt to get Earnhardt to drive those 11 races. But then Wrangler Jeans, Earnhardt's sponsor when he was driving for Stacy, offered to sponsor Earnhardt under Richard Childress Racing too.

Earnhardt drove his 11 races for Childress in the 1981 season, and six times he finished in the top ten. However, though Earnhardt and Childress got along well, Childress's team was still young and struggling with money issues. Earnhardt had offers to drive for other teams, so he and Childress agreed that it was best if Earnhardt took up one of those offers. Earnhardt decided to drive for Bud Moore Engineering. He stayed with Moore for two years, but in that time he did not finish many of the races he drove in, and when he did finish he was well back in the standings. He won only three races. After the 1983 season, Earnhardt signed with Childress again, and he would stay with Childress for the rest of his career. The NASCAR star would win six of his seven championships as part of Richard Childress Racing.

Built from the Ground Up

Richard Childress Racing designs and builds its race cars from the ground up, rather than just modifying cars or using parts built by someone else. Childress has always felt that the only way to win is to build cars this way. The crew members engineer and then build their own frame and suspension, design and build the car bodies, and build and test their own engines. They use computers to simulate race conditions and then modify their cars to be more aerodynamic, testing and retesting them in a wind tunnel. While this kind of car technology and construction is very expensive, it has paid off for Childress in wins. In early 2020, his enterprise included eight full-time race teams, hundreds of employees, and a large facility with an engineering staff.[6]

▲ Throughout his career, Earnhardt earned more than $40 million.

The Pass in the Grass

It was 1987, and Earnhardt was racing in the NASCAR All-Star Race at Charlotte Motor Speedway when he executed a racing maneuver that would later be called the "pass in the grass."[7]

It cemented Earnhardt's reputation as the Intimidator. Earnhardt, Bill Elliott, and Geoff Bodine were all fighting for the lead, and there had been several instances of the cars bumping each other. With eight laps to go in the race, Elliott gave Earnhardt's car a bump coming out of a turn, sending Earnhardt sliding across the track and into the grass strip between the track and the pit lane. However, Earnhardt kept control of his car and never slowed down, moving through the grass and right back onto the track. Earnhardt won the race, but both Elliott and Bodine were so angry at the way Earnhardt had continually bumped them that they rammed his car after it crossed the finish line.

All three drivers were fined by NASCAR for their maneuvers on the racetrack that day, but Earnhardt's

The Pit Crew Team

A good pit crew is essential to any racing team because the crew handles all of the jobs needed to keep the car running at its best during a race. Earnhardt's long-time pit crew consisted of four men. Danny "Chocolate" Myers refueled Earnhardt's car. David Smith used a jack to elevate the car for tire changes. Will Lind changed the tires, and Danny Lawrence tuned the engine. These four men stayed with Earnhardt through his entire career once he signed with Childress.

When Andy Petree took over as crew chief in 1993, he wanted his new team members to walk him through their process. Surely they had some tricks up their sleeves that made them so successful. Instead, Lind explained that the driver was the key to the team's success. "Right here in the seat is all of our tricks—right here. . . . We got nothing . . . but Dale Earnhardt. He was the trick," said Lind.[8]

▲ If cars bump into each other on the racetrack, hazardous accidents can happen.

reputation had only grown. The pass in the grass would become one of his most famous moments. As Humpy Wheeler, the former president of the Charlotte Motor Speedway, said, "The greatest move in the history of auto racing. To be driving a car that fast on the grass? To keep control? That was unbelievable."[9]

Another decision made that year would also become part of the Earnhardt legend. His blue-and-yellow No. 3 car with Childress Racing changed when Wrangler stopped sponsoring the team. Instead, GM Goodwrench began sponsoring Earnhardt. As a result, his car was painted black. The black No. 3 car would become

Motor Racing Outreach

In the 1990s, Earnhardt became active in a religious ministry called Motor Racing Outreach, run by Rev. Max Helton. It began in 1988, when Helton began holding Sunday morning services for the drivers and their crews at NASCAR races. Helton remembered Earnhardt:

> *I found him to be very thoughtful of other people. Very kind and generous. Around '93 or '94, a couple of drivers asked me to pray with them before races. I agreed, but got to thinking that I really shouldn't be showing favoritism to anyone. So I announced that I was available for any driver to pray before a race. Dale was the first to say, 'Yeah, I'd like that.' It kind of surprised me at the time, because I didn't know him that well and there was all of the Intimidator reputation . . . but privately he was much different."*[10]

▲ Earnhardt took home the win after his pass in the grass.

Earnhardt's identity for the rest of his career, and he became known as the Man in Black.

6
Rough Roads

Things had been going well for Earnhardt. He had a solid relationship with Richard Childress Racing. In 1982 he got married to Teresa Houston. And Earnhardt was winning races and making money. But beginning in 1987, there were rougher roads for Earnhardt.

Following the race with the pass in the grass, the NASCAR chief executive received a letter from one of Bill Elliott's fans. In it, the fan threatened to kill Earnhardt for his "dirty driving."[1] The Federal Bureau of Investigation

▸ Teresa went to races with Earnhardt and supported his career.

GM
odwrench
Service Plus

(FBI) was alerted about the letter, and it sent agents to the locations of Earnhardt's next few races. Agents were instructed to be with Earnhardt at all times, and other agents were stationed among the spectators. Local police were also alerted. However, the races were run without any problems, and eventually the FBI called off the investigation.

A Near Win

In February 1990, Earnhardt was still chasing that elusive first win at the Daytona 500. Earnhardt's Chevrolet was in front of the pack for much of the race, leading on 155 of the 200 laps, and he led by more than half a lap near the end of the race. Then, on the last lap, something hit Earnhardt's right rear tire, mangling it. "I hit some debris, I don't know what," Earnhardt said. "I heard it hit the bottom of the car and then it hit the tire. That's when it popped."[2] Four drivers passed Earnhardt before he reached the checkered flag. The fifth-place finish was a bitter disappointment after coming so close to winning his first Daytona 500.

In 1992, Earnhardt won only one race. He bounced back in 1993, when he won a sixth Winston Cup championship. In 1994, he drove in 31 races and won four, in addition to finishing

▲ Winning the Daytona 500 is something many racers strive to achieve.

in the top ten 25 times. It was enough to win a seventh Winston Cup title, tying him with the legendary Richard Petty for the most Winston Cup championships. The next year, Earnhardt won five races but lost the overall championship to Jeff Gordon. Earnhardt started the 1996 season with two wins in his first four races, and he was leading in points coming into the July 28, 1996, race at the Talladega Superspeedway racetrack in Talladega, Alabama.

A Restricted Track

The 1996 DieHard 500 Winston Cup race was set to begin, but it had been raining heavily, soaking the 2.6-mile (4.2 km) track and the grassy areas around it. The scheduled start time had already been delayed because conditions on the track were too wet for racing. When the rain finally let up enough for racing to begin, the first 12 laps took place under a yellow flag, keeping the cars' speeds lower until the track had a chance to dry out.

Talladega, along with Daytona, is one of the two fastest NASCAR tracks. These tracks are fast because they have long straight sections where cars can reach high speeds, and large curves with high banking that allows drivers to turn at a faster speed. Banking means that the turns are higher on the outside of the track and lower toward the center.

Because of the fast track, NASCAR required all the cars at the DieHard 500 to be fitted with carburetor restrictor plates. These safety devices are designed to slow the race cars down and prevent high-speed crashes. However, drivers complain that they can also create a safety hazard because they cause the cars to all go similar speeds. This can create packs of cars. And if one

▲ Racing in packs can quickly turn dangerous if there's a crash.

car crashes, it usually causes others to crash too, leading to pileups. In that 1996 race, carburetor restrictor plates caused dozens of cars to get bunched up behind the leader.

Crash on the 117th Lap

Earnhardt, in his black No. 3 Chevrolet, was competing with Jeff Gordon and Sterling Marlin for the lead. The jockeying continued among the field of cars, with Earnhardt using his familiar tactics to take the lead. But on Lap 117, the right front of Ernie Irvan's car touched the left rear of Marlin's car, sending Marlin into Earnhardt. Both cars ended up taking a right-hand turn directly into the wall.

Earnhardt's car hit the wall, bounced off it, turned upside down, and was then hit hard by two other cars before coming to a stop farther down the track. "When the car turned abruptly sideways, I knew I was going to hit the wall," Earnhardt later said. "When it hit the wall is when I broke my sternum. When the car got on [its] side and got up in the air a little bit, it was spinning around. I seen a flash and another car hit me at the same time. . . . There was a big crash and the car went airborne again."[3]

Fire and smoke were shooting out of the engine compartment. Earnhardt switched off the car's engine, since the wiring was burning. The safety crews arrived and helped pull him from the car.

Earnhardt refused a stretcher, to the amazement of the press and the cheers of the fans. Everyone thought he was badly injured. But Earnhardt later admitted it wasn't a sign of toughness. "I wanted to lay down," he said.

▲ Spectators watched and waited for news about Earnhardt's condition after the crash.

▲ EARNHARDT DOMINATED NASCAR RACING IN THE 1980S AND 1990S.

"I didn't want to stand up, but I had to because it hurt too bad to lay down, so I said, 'Just walk me to the ambulance.'"[4] He was later diagnosed with a broken sternum, broken collarbone, and bruised pelvis. Other drivers said it was about the worst crash that a driver could be in and still survive.

The 50 Greatest

In 1998, to celebrate its 50th anniversary, NASCAR created a list of its 50 greatest drivers of all time. When the results were announced, NASCAR President Bill France Jr. said, "These are the men who define the competition of our sport. Their accomplishments are the benchmark that much of our history is identified by. . . . These are the drivers who made and make NASCAR fans stand on their feet and cheer. These are the drivers who are NASCAR history."[5] Earnhardt was on the list, along with his father.

One result of Earnhardt's crash was the required installation of a new roll bar. The bar would be placed in the roll cage of metal tubing that surrounds the driver inside the car. This new bar ran from the top to the bottom of the windshield in the middle, providing additional protection in the long expanse between the left and right sides of the roll cage. A bar like this could have prevented some of Earnhardt's injuries in his crash. It was nicknamed the Earnhardt bar.

Down but Not Out

Earnhardt's crash at Talladega occurred just when the racing legend was heating up. Before the accident, Earnhardt had already won two races and was leading in points for the Winston Cup championship. The crash at Talladega put an end to Earnhardt's hopes for a chance to win an eighth season title.

But Earnhardt had a strong record of coming back from losses, crashes, and equipment failures. And more than anything, Earnhardt was determined. Just one week after his Talladega accident, his injuries made it difficult for him to breathe or raise his right arm. But he still completed six laps of a race at the Indianapolis Motor Speedway before letting his relief driver Mike Skinner

Driving with Injuries

NASCAR doctor Jerry Punch recalled what happened when people tried to talk Earnhardt out of racing weeks after his crash at Talladega:

> *[Earnhardt] couldn't raise his left arm and he couldn't breathe. . . . Richard [Childress] and Teresa [Earnhardt] were getting me to help convince him to not get in the car, for his own safety. He looked right at Richard and said, 'If you tell me, Richard, I'm going to hurt this race team by being in your race car, I won't get in it.' Richard said, 'Are you kidding me? You're Dale Earnhardt. I can't tell you you're going to hurt my race team by being in my car.' And Dale said, 'All right, it's done.'*[6]

Earnhardt raced around the track, sometimes using his knees to steer. He shifted and often steered with one hand. He completed the race at Watkins Glen and came in sixth. "It hurts," he said then. "But it's a good hurt."[7]

take over. A week after that, he competed at a New York road racing course called Watkins Glen International. Unlike an oval NASCAR track, this course twisted and turned like a regular road, making it necessary for the driver to do a lot of shifting and turning of the wheel.

Earnhardt had survived a crash that could have easily killed him. However, his recovery took time. The following season, in 1997, he did not record a single win. This was only the second time in his racing career that had happened. He also had some unexplained medical issues. But despite all of these setbacks, Earnhardt opened the 1998 season with his first Daytona 500 in February. The Man in Black was once again on top.

Aftereffects of the Crash?

On August 31, 1997, Earnhardt was starting the Southern 500 in Darlington, South Carolina, when he seemed to black out. Disoriented, he hit the wall on the first turn, then slowly drove around the track twice looking for the pit road. Childress reached him on the car radio and ordered him to come in. "I'm sorry, I saw two racetracks," Earnhardt finally responded.[8] Childress replaced him with another driver. Later that day Earnhardt seemed to have no memory of what had happened. He was thoroughly checked out at the hospital, and doctors found nothing that could have caused the blackout. However, some people think it could have been part of the aftereffects of his serious crash at Talladega in 1996.

7

The Last Lap

It was a clear day on February 18, 2001—the day of the forty-third Daytona 500 race. The morning would start off with the drivers' meeting that always preceded a race. These meetings are attended by drivers and crew chiefs and are the last chance to review race procedures and rules, speed limits, pit road access, and other details that the drivers need to know.

Earnhardt would be racing that day for Childress. His son Dale Jr. and driver Michael Waltrip drove for Earnhardt's own racing

▸ THE DAYTONA INTERNATIONAL SPEEDWAY IS ONE OF THE BIGGEST STADIUMS IN THE COUNTRY.

DAYTONA
INTERNATIONAL SPEEDWAY
TOURS DAILY

company, Dale Earnhardt Inc. (DEI), which Earnhardt had started in 1998. Dale Jr. had followed in his dad's footsteps to become a driver. By 1998 he had started filling in for other drivers at DEI, and before long he was good enough to race full time.

Ty Norris, an executive for DEI, remembered meeting with Earnhardt that morning:

> *We met every day in his [RV]. He always sat at this little table in a dining area. We sat across from each other. He was wearing a black shirt and jeans—his Sunday attire. Then he would put on a leather jacket to go to the drivers' meeting. He was very positive that day. Michael [Waltrip] had shown so much speed that week. He felt like one of us would win—either himself, Michael, or Junior. He specifically said, 'We can win this race today.'*[1]

After the meeting, Waltrip walked to the track with Earnhardt. "He hit me on the back and said, 'You know what to do.' And he walked away," recalled Waltrip.[2]

In the Front of the Pack

Earnhardt's black No. 3 car, as well as the three other cars that he owned, were doing well for most of the race. Because of the use of restrictor plates, the cars were frequently bunched up, making maneuvering difficult, and there was a great deal of bumping and cutting other cars off. Earnhardt was in the lead on the 27th lap out of 200, and he held that position for 11 laps. He eventually lost his lead, then regained it for laps 83 and 84. For much of the race, Earnhardt and the other drivers in his group were running at the front of the pack.

Waltrip said, "The race started, and I chilled out and took my time. We were running 1, 2, 3, 4. It was amazing because, the night before, Dale predicted it when we had this impromptu meeting. I liked what he was saying, but I thought it might be a little unrealistic. I mean, there are going to be 40 other cars. And me, him, and Dale Jr. are gonna win it? But it's Dale. Then during the race, I saw Dale behind me and I thought, . . . 'How'd he know?'"[3]

The 500

Since 1982, the Daytona 500 race has been the official start to the NASCAR racing season. It is also considered to be the most prestigious and important race in NASCAR. Winners can take home prize money of $1 million or more.[4]

The Daytona 500 race is not a 500-lap race. The number *500* refers to the total number of miles of the race. Since every lap is 2.5 miles (4 km) in length, it takes 200 laps to equal 500 miles (805 km). The race itself should only take about 2.5 hours to drive, but with pit stops, cautions, and weather delays, it can actually last much longer.

BUMPER CARS

On the 174th lap, the race positions once again reflected the downside of racing with restrictor plates. Cars began hitting each other like bumper cars in a carnival ride. Driver Robby Gordon hit Ward Burton, which made Burton hit Tony Stewart. Stewart's car spun and flipped, hitting Bobby Labonte. Ultimately, 19 cars were involved in the accident, which looked more serious than it proved to be. Earnhardt was ahead of the accident, and after the track was cleared and the race was restarted on the 180th lap, he was second behind his son. He then fell to third behind Waltrip. There were only five laps left in the race, and things were looking good for Earnhardt and his drivers.

Earnhardt seemed to be concerned that

Drafting

On the racetrack, cars use an aerodynamic principle called drafting to help them move more quickly. When a race car moves very fast, air flows over and under it. More airflow over the top of the car causes something called negative lift, which basically helps the car stick to the track because the air is pressing it down. But all that air flowing around the car also creates something called drag, which slows the car down. There is an advantage to the car traveling very closely—often just a few inches—behind a lead car, because that lead car has broken through the air in front of it and reduces the drag for the car right behind it. This is drafting, and it can increase the speed of the following car by about five miles per hour (8 kmh).[5]

▲ EARNHARDT AND DALE JR., *RIGHT*, OFTEN RACED AGAINST EACH OTHER.

other cars would take advantage of the draft his car was producing to speed past him, Waltrip, and Dale Jr. at the last moment. This had happened several times during the previous season. So he decided to block for the two leading cars to keep them from being overtaken. Earnhardt advised his son and Waltrip to drive on the lower part of the racetrack, and he put himself into the blocking position in the middle of the track, slowing down just enough to keep the cars behind him from getting by. Then, they entered the final turn of the race.

THE CRASH

Drivers Ken Schrader and Sterling Marlin were driving the way any competitive driver would—trying to get past Earnhardt coming into the final turn of the race. Marlin moved his car low on the track to try to get past the lead cars. Earnhardt moved left to block Marlin and clipped Marlin's right front bumper. The impact turned Earnhardt's car toward the center apron of the track. As Earnhardt tried to recover from the bump, the car zoomed back up the track toward the wall, right in front of Schrader's car. Earnhardt's No. 3 Chevrolet hit the wall going 180 miles per hour (290 kmh), and Schrader's car hit him on the passenger side.[6]

Driver Rusty Wallace remembered thinking the crash hadn't been that bad. "I see Dale and he goes flying across the front of me. I'll never forget his car just flying across the bow. I just chirped off the throttle. It was not a bad wreck. I remember thinking, 'Oh man is he gonna be [angry].'"[7]

Shortly after the crash, Waltrip ended up winning the race, with Dale Jr. coming in second.

▲ EARNHARDT WAS FIGHTING FOR THIRD PLACE WHEN THE CRASH HAPPENED.

Meanwhile, Earnhardt's car had rolled down the track and onto the grass after the impact. Schrader had gotten out of his car and was the first one to reach Earnhardt. He lifted the netting over the driver's window and then began waving his hands wildly for the emergency crew. The emergency truck arrived moments later.

Schrader didn't talk about what he'd seen inside the car until many years later, when he said that he knew Earnhardt was dead. Schrader said, "I didn't want to be the one who said, 'Dale is dead.' The hardest thing I ever had to do was face Richard [Childress] in the infield care center after the crash. He pulled the curtain back and asked what was going on. I told him it was bad. He wanted to know if Dale was going to be out for a while and I looked at him and said, 'No Richard, it's really bad.' I couldn't say it."[8]

The Announcement

Earnhardt had always been incredibly tough when it came to crashes, and most of the people watching the race expected him to climb out of the wrecked car and give a wave as he limped to an ambulance. But instead, they saw Earnhardt being put onto a stretcher and hauled into an ambulance. When the ambulance drove away, some observers noticed it wasn't moving very fast.

Earnhardt was taken to Halifax Medical Center in Daytona Beach. He was pronounced dead at 5:16 p.m. He died from a severe fracture to the base of his skull, and he likely died the moment he hit the racetrack wall.

It was three hours before NASCAR made the official announcement. Mike Helton, the president of NASCAR, said, with his voice breaking, "We've lost Dale Earnhardt."[9]

Hawks

The day after Earnhardt's death, ten hawks were seen circling the spot above the Daytona racetrack where Earnhardt had crashed. Nine of the hawks flew in a circle, but the tenth one dove down to almost the exact spot of the crash, then back up to the circle, then down again, over and over. Two sportswriters saw the birds' odd behavior. One of them, Mike Vega, said, "You start thinking. You know, maybe the hawks in the air are the other guys who have died. Neil Bonnett. Adam Petty. All those guys. And the hawk that keeps diving, coming back to the spot, maybe that's [Dale]."[10]

8

The Aftermath

On Wednesday, February 21, 2001, Earnhardt's family held a private burial service. The next day, invited guests gathered at Calvary Church in Charlotte, North Carolina, for a celebration of Earnhardt's life. The Earnhardt family attended, as did his racing team, sponsors, officials from NASCAR, drivers in the Winston Cup, and employees from DEI. In total, an estimated 3,000 people were in attendance.[1] The service was also televised nationwide. The day was cold and rainy, but that didn't keep Earnhardt's fans from

▸ Some people paid their respects to Earnhardt by placing flowers on a black race car.

GM
Service
Plus

▲ Some racing venues, such as the Las Vegas Motor Speedway, created tributes for the NASCAR star.

gathering outside the church. Many had driven hours to get there.

"We Will Miss Him Terribly"

Driver Rusty Wallace was one of those who spoke at the service, standing next to an arrangement of white, black, and red carnations shaped like Earnhardt's No. 3. "None of us were ready to let Dale go, and we will miss him terribly,"

Wallace said. "God created only one Dale Earnhardt and no one will ever replace him, neither in our sport or in our hearts."[2]

The short service ended when Teresa Earnhardt and her daughter, Taylor, made their way up onto the podium. Teresa turned toward the section where the other Winston Cup drivers were sitting and blew them a kiss. "Thank you," she whispered.[3]

Fans wanted to remember Earnhardt at every racing venue as the season continued. At racetracks all over the country, there were moments of silence, military planes flying low in the air, and fans holding three fingers up to the sky for every third lap, because of Earnhardt's No. 3. There were other tributes, such as floral arrangements and No. 3s painted on track walls. Tributes to Earnhardt would dominate the 2001 NASCAR season.

Finding Fault

As the racing world paid tribute to Earnhardt, NASCAR was investigating why the accident happened and why Earnhardt died. The Volusia County, Florida, medical examiner, Dr. Thomas Beaver, was the first to release the exact cause of Earnhardt's death after an autopsy. According to medical professionals, Earnhardt died when his

Safety

Former NASCAR Winston Cup director Gary Nelson commented on a change in Earnhardt before his death. He noted that for years Earnhardt had been focused on speed while racing and that he resisted the idea of additional safety measures. But before his death, Earnhardt had asked Nelson to visit his shop. There, he walked Nelson through some ideas he had to make safer cars for his racers.

head was whipped forward violently on impact. His neck muscles weren't able to keep his neck from snapping away from the base of his skull. The autopsy report also found that Earnhardt's chin had hit the steering wheel hard enough to bend it, and that that blow alone would have been enough to kill him.

Some people speculated that Earnhardt's head had been able to whip forward because of a malfunctioning seat belt—which in a race car is actually a five-point harness, not just a lap belt as in a passenger car—or because that seat belt had been improperly installed, catching on a metal guide at the left of his seat and throwing him into the steering wheel and then back into his seat.

NASCAR later claimed that the seat belt had malfunctioned. NASCAR president Mike Helton noted that the webbing on the seat belt had broken, and he suggested Earnhardt might have survived the crash if it had been intact and held him in place. However, another unnamed source claimed that Earnhardt had altered the seat belt somehow in order to make himself more comfortable in the car, as racers often did with equipment. Earnhardt had a reputation for not being concerned about safety equipment.

A DRIVER TO BLAME?

In the aftermath of Earnhardt's deadly accident, people also pointed their fingers at the actions of the other drivers in the race, especially Sterling Marlin, whose bump pushed Earnhardt's car into the wall. Marlin and his family received death threats by phone, and he even had to shut down his website temporarily because of the number of negative

Ken Schrader

In a 2020 podcast, Ken Schrader and Dale Earnhardt Jr. discussed Schrader's experience as the first one to reach Earnhardt Sr.'s car following the crash. In 19 years, Schrader had never told anyone just what he saw that day. Dale Jr. ended the podcast by reading a note he'd written to Schrader:

> *I've known you a long time and a lot of time has passed since that happened. And you've been a great friend to me. You're one of only a few to see the darkest moment for my dad. Though you have intimate knowledge of those moments, you are a keeper of that delicate information. It makes me feel close to you, Kenny. I feel pain for you to have to carry that memory, but you carry it for me . . . you carry it for anyone who's ever cheered for him. It's a secret that you'll keep 'til your last breath. Kenny, I know you might sometimes wish you weren't the one, but I'm glad it was you.*[4]

comments and emails he was receiving. Dale Earnhardt Jr. came to Marlin's defense, saying, "Any notion, or any idea or any blame placed upon anyone, whether it be Sterling Marlin or anyone else for that matter, it's ridiculous."[5]

Marlin spoke out about a conversation he'd had with Earnhardt just a month before the crash, talking about the possibility of dying in a race. "Dale said, 'If I ever get killed in a race car . . . I don't want nobody crying and moaning and groaning. . . . It's what I love to do, and don't worry about it,'" Marlin noted.[6]

CHANGES

As a result of Earnhardt's crash and death, NASCAR made safety changes to race cars and racetracks. One change was installing softer crash walls on tracks, made with material that helps to dissipate energy. Other changes included safety equipment within cars, such as adding protective seats, better roll cages, roof hatches for escaping the car, and elements inside the car's frame that are made from energy-absorbing materials. New rules were established about seat placement and better seat belt systems. Drivers today now have to wear a head and neck restraint device. This device, called the HANS device, was one of the major changes to come from Earnhardt's death.

▲ NASCAR SAFETY EQUIPMENT, SUCH AS HARNESSES, CONTINUE TO BE UPDATED.

It is a semihard neck collar that fastens to the driver's upper body by a harness. The collar has two flexible tethers, or straps, that keep the driver's head from snapping forward or sideways during an impact.

Ricky Craven, a former race car driver, said of Earnhardt's death, "I believe it required us to study longer, work harder, and understand what the limitations of the human body are and really study the impacts, not only on the car but residual effects on the body."[7]

Earnhardt's death also marked a point of change for NASCAR itself. NASCAR racing was no longer the way it had been for Earnhardt, where drivers drove as fast as possible, bumped each other's cars, and didn't always follow the rules or wear all the suggested safety equipment. NASCAR instead began to

Making Changes

Earnhardt's death was not the only tragedy that cast a spotlight on problems with NASCAR's safety efforts. In 2000, Adam Petty, son of driver Kyle Petty and grandson of racing legend Richard Petty, was killed at New Hampshire Motor Speedway when the accelerator of his car stuck and he crashed into a wall at more than 130 miles per hour (210 kmh).[8] He died instantly. In the next nine months, three more drivers died in racing accidents.

Petty's death, like Earnhardt's a year later, resulted in NASCAR safety changes. In Petty's case it was a ruling that all cars must have a button that instantly turns off the engine. However, during this string of deaths there was the opinion that NASCAR had been far too slow to implement safety regulations and technology compared to governance in other kinds of motorsports.

▲ People across the country mourned the loss of the spectacular NASCAR driver.

focus more on safety, such as slowing cars down so that races are closer and more exciting. In 2019, no NASCAR driver had died as a result of a crash since Earnhardt's death.

9

Remembering Dale Earnhardt Sr.

In the first weeks after Earnhardt's death, shrines were created at the Daytona racetrack and other tracks, where fans could leave flowers, mementos, and messages. The Daytona shrine was created outside Gate 82, the closest spot to where Earnhardt's accident took place. Fans also encouraged other tracks to hold memorial services for Earnhardt. According to Jeff Byrd, the president of Bristol Motor Speedway, where Earnhardt won his first professional race, "We [had] to do something. The switchboards [were]

▸ One of Earnhardt's lasting legacies is his children. Dale Jr. won his second Daytona 500 in 2014.

2014
THE
Harley J. Earl DAYTONA 500 Trophy
NATIONAL GUARD
Hendrick MOTORSPORTS
GOODYEAR
Mtn Dew
NASCAR Sprint CUP SERIES
DAYTONA 500
2014
THE GREAT AMERICAN RACE
56TH ANNUAL

going crazy. The emails [kept] coming. People needed a place to go."[1] They put up a wall at the track where people could leave messages, and a short memorial service was held. The crowd in attendance was estimated at 5,000 to 6,000 people.[2] Memorials like these took place at NASCAR tracks all over the country.

Although fans have continued to remember Earnhardt over the years and mark the anniversaries of his death and birthday, there have also been more substantial tributes to Earnhardt's legacy. In 2002,

Dale Jr. and Jeffrey Earnhardt

Both Dale Jr. and his nephew Jeffrey Earnhardt have had careers in racing. Dale Jr. never reached the level of success as his dad, but he did win 26 Cup Series races and two Daytona 500s.[3] One memorable win happened at the Pepsi 400 on the Daytona track just months after his father's death. Moments after Dale Jr.'s win, a broadcaster said, "Some of the moves he made on the track today—looked like his father behind the wheel."[4]

Jeffrey started NASCAR racing in 2009 and was still racing in early 2020. He's competed in both Xfinity Series and Cup Series races. Like his uncle Dale Jr., he's faced pressure having the Earnhardt name. There are some people who have claimed that Dale Jr. and Jeffrey have only gotten opportunities because of their famous last name. In 2019, Jeffrey spoke with Dale Jr. about this pressure. "Obviously, expectations are high, and people automatically assume just because of your last name, you're gonna win races. And unfortunately, wins don't come that easy," said Jeffrey. He later added, "I'm cutting my own path. I'm not you, I'm not Pawpaw Dale."[5]

the nonprofit Dale Earnhardt Foundation was created. Its mission is to continue Earnhardt's legacy through charitable programs and grants, especially those that support children, education, and environmental preservation—issues that were very important to Earnhardt during his lifetime. The foundation has supported projects such as planting trees and funding green schools, where students are taught about environmental sustainability. It has also helped provide food to children and families who need it, has given books to homeless shelters, and has established a scholarship for college undergraduates who are interested in motorsports and automotive engineering.

Earnhardt received many honors and awards after his death. He was inducted into the International Motorsports Hall of Fame in 2006, and he was part of the first group enshrined in the NASCAR Hall of Fame in 2010. Also in 2010, the North Carolina Motorsports Association announced that Earnhardt would be the 2010 Achievement in Motorsports Tribute Award recipient. Earnhardt's helmet from the 1998 season is also on display at the Smithsonian National Museum of American History in Washington, DC.

▲ Earnhardt's children and widow went to the Hall of Fame ceremony where Earnhardt was honored.

THE DALE TRAIL

For fans who want to connect with Earnhardt's legacy, there are certain places they can visit to remember him. There is an official Dale Trail, a self-guided route that covers landmarks in Kannapolis and Mooresville, North Carolina, that relate to Earnhardt and his family.

The route begins on Dale Earnhardt Boulevard, off Interstate 95 north of Charlotte. Earnhardt's grave cannot be visited, because he was buried at the back of his private estate property. But Earnhardt's company headquarters, located in Mooresville, receives tour buses filled with visitors every day.

DEI no longer exists as a racing team. Its headquarters is now mostly a museum, events venue, and store. The museum has all seven of Earnhardt's Winston Cup championship trophies, as well as items such as his old racing suits and a few cars. The facility also includes the corporate

DEI

In 2008 DEI merged with Chip Ganassi Racing to form the Earnhardt Ganassi Racing Team. It is now based in a shop near Concord, North Carolina. The Earnhardt Childress Racing engine shop is located in Welcome, North Carolina. Teresa Earnhardt gave a statement after the opening of the Earnhardt Childress Racing shop. She emphasized that it was not just a museum to her husband or another corporate headquarters: "It's still a race shop. It'll always be a race shop."[6] There have been plans to start racing under the DEI name again, with Earnhardt's grandson Jeffrey driving.

offices for the Dale Earnhardt Foundation as well as several other related businesses.

Other places have been named or renamed in honor of Earnhardt, such as the Earnhardt Towers building at the Darlington Raceway in South Carolina. The building includes grandstands as well as a media center and offices, and the trackside parts of the building have Earnhardt's name on them. Graphics on the back side of the towers show events from both Dale Sr. and Dale Jr.'s careers.

Ride the Intimidator

At Kings Dominion amusement park in Doswell, Virginia, the Intimidator 305 roller coaster opened in 2010. It was named after Earnhardt and features train cars that looked like Earnhardt's No. 3 Chevrolet. The ride features a 300-foot (90 m) drop and is known for its high-speed twists and turns.[7] Carowinds amusement park in Charlotte also has an Intimidator coaster, which is more than 200 feet (60 m) tall and reaches speeds of 80 mph (130 kmh).[8] Both coasters feature entrances with replicas of Earnhardt's famous car and information about his life and career.

The Lasting Legacy

Of course, Earnhardt's most lasting legacy is his family: his children and grandchildren. His son Dale Jr. had a successful racing career of his own prior to retiring in 2017. Earnhardt's grandson Jeffrey is now racing.

Earnhardt was an aggressive and sometimes intimidating opponent on the racetrack. But he worked hard to become what he was. He had his share of losses, crashes, and disappointments, but he

▲ Earnhardt memorabilia, such as race cars he drove, are in racing museums.

▲ The city of Kannapolis put up a nine-foot (2.7 m) statue of Earnhardt to memorialize him.

kept pushing through the difficult times. In the end, Earnhardt won 76 Winston Cup races and seven NASCAR season championships.[9] He is thought of as one of the best racers NASCAR has ever seen. Earnhardt's determination is reflected in one of his famous quotes about racing: "The winner ain't the one with the fastest car; it's the one who refuses to lose."[10]

Timeline

1951	1968	1969
On April 29, Ralph Dale Earnhardt Sr. is born.	Earnhardt marries his first wife, Latane Brown.	Earnhardt's son Kerry is born.

1974	1975	1977
Dale Jr. is born.	Earnhardt competes at the Charlotte Motor Speedway and finishes twenty-second in the race.	Earnhardt and Brenda divorce.

1970	1971	1972
Earnhardt and Latane divorce.	Earnhardt competes in his first auto race.	Earnhardt marries Brenda Gee, and their daughter, Kelley, is born.

1978	1980	1981
Earnhardt joins Rod Osterlund Racing.	Earnhardt wins his first Winston Cup championship.	Earnhardt begins racing for Richard Childress.

TIMELINE

1982	1987	1990
Earnhardt marries Teresa Houston.	During the All-Star Race, Earnhardt does his famous pass in the grass.	During the Daytona 500, Earnhardt runs over a piece of debris that cuts his tire and costs him the win.

2001	2001	2001
On February 18, Earnhardt crashes into a wall head-on at the Daytona 500 and is declared dead.	On February 22, a memorial service is held for Earnhardt at Calvary Church in Charlotte, North Carolina.	Following Earnhardt's death, NASCAR begins to look into new safety measures for its drivers.

1994	1996	1998
Earnhardt wins his seventh Winston Cup championship.	At the DieHard 500, Earnhardt has a serious accident. It leads NASCAR to require all cars to install a roll bar for safety.	On February 15, Earnhardt wins his first Daytona 500 race.

2002	2006	2010
The Dale Earnhardt Foundation is created.	Earnhardt is posthumously admitted into the International Motorsports Hall of Fame.	Earnhardt posthumously receives the Achievement in Motorsports Tribute Award.

ESSENTIAL FACTS

DATE OF BIRTH

April 29, 1951

PLACE OF BIRTH

Kannapolis, North Carolina

PARENTS

Ralph and Martha Earnhardt

EDUCATION

Attended high school through age 16; did not graduate

MARRIAGE

Latane Brown (1968–1970);
Brenda Gee (1972–1977);
Teresa Houston (1982–2001)

CHILDREN

Kerry, Kelley, Dale Jr., and Taylor

CAREER HIGHLIGHTS

Dale Earnhardt Sr. was one of the best drivers in NASCAR history, winning 76 Winston Cup races during his career as well as the 1998 Daytona 500. He also won seven Winston Cup championships and the 1979 Rookie of the Year award. He was named one of NASCAR's 50 Greatest Drivers in 1998 and was inducted into the NASCAR Hall of Fame's first class in 2010.

SOCIETAL CONTRIBUTION

Earnhardt's racing company, Dale Earnhardt Inc. (DEI), helped bring talented drivers to the racetrack. Earnhardt also touched the lives of many loyal fans, who flooded NASCAR with memorials and tributes after the famous racer's sudden death. The Dale Earnhardt Foundation also helps the community and keeps the NASCAR driver's legacy alive.

CONFLICTS

Earnhardt's love of racing put pressure on his finances and family early in his career. In addition, his aggressive driving style didn't always make him friends on the racetrack. Once, after a particularly heated race, two drivers purposefully crashed into Earnhardt's car as payback for his moves on the track.

QUOTE

"It's a feeling you can't replace. It's eluded us for so many years. . . . I never believed, when guys told me how good it felt to win the 500. I never believed it, but I do now. It sure feels good."

—Dale Earnhardt Sr. on his first Daytona 500 win

GLOSSARY

aerodynamic
Having a shape that keeps air from dragging as it moves across.

apron
A paved section around the bottom of a track that is not supposed to be used for racing.

autopsy
The examination of a body after death to determine the cause of death.

carburetor
A part of an internal combustion engine that mixes fuel with air.

circuit
An established schedule of events in racing.

concussion
A brain injury from a hard hit to the head.

jockey
To struggle in order to gain or achieve something.

lap
One full run around a racetrack.

pace car
A car that leads other race cars and sets a racing speed in hazardous situations.

pit crew
The people whose job during a race is to keep the car in top condition, including refueling a race car, replacing tires, and making repairs.

pit lane
A lane beside a racetrack where racing teams have their garages; also called the pit road.

posthumously
Happening after someone's death.

qualifying
Meeting standards to participate at a certain level.

sponsor
An organization or corporation that provides the money for a group or cause, often in exchange for advertising.

stock car
A car that is based on a normal car but has undergone modifications for racing.

SELECTED BIBLIOGRAPHY

Crossman, Matt. "A Daytona Legend." *NASCAR*, 15 Feb. 2018, nascar.com. Accessed 3 Apr. 2020.

Gillispie, Tom. *Angel in Black: Memories of Dale Earnhardt Sr.* Cumberland House, 2007.

Montville, Leigh. *At the Altar of Speed: The Fast Life and Tragic Death of Dale Earnhardt*. Doubleday, 2001.

FURTHER READINGS

Fielden, Greg, and Bryan Hallman. *NASCAR: The Complete History*. Publications International, 2018.

Ventura, Marne. *STEM in the Daytona 500*. Abdo, 2020.

ONLINE RESOURCES

To learn more about Dale Earnhardt Sr., please visit **abdobooklinks.com** or scan this QR code. These links are routinely monitored and updated to provide the most current information available.

MORE INFORMATION

For more information on this subject, contact or visit the following organizations:

Dale Earnhardt Inc.
1675 Coddle Creek Hwy.
Mooresville, NC 28115
704-662-8000
daleearnhardtinc.com
Visitors to Dale Earnhardt Inc. can see a museum and showroom, visit the store, and learn about special events throughout the year. It is also the headquarters for the Dale Earnhardt Foundation and several other DEI businesses.

Motorsports Hall of Fame of America
1801 West International Speedway Blvd.
Daytona Beach, FL 32114
386-200-9349
mshf.com
The Motorsports Hall of Fame honors all motorsports, such as racing cars, motorcycles, and power boats. It also has a museum located at the Daytona International Speedway.

Source Notes

Chapter 1. The Race of a Lifetime

1. Matt Crossman. "A Daytona Legend." *NASCAR*, 15 Feb. 2018, nascar.com. Accessed 19 May 2020.

2. Bob Pockrass. "Dale Earnhardt's Daytona 500 Win Has Unique Place in NASCAR History." *ESPN*, 15 Feb. 2018, espn.com. Accessed 19 May 2020.

3. Brendan Marks. "Dale Earnhardt Won Daytona 500 with Her Lucky Penny Glued to Dash. That Moment Endures." *Charlotte Observer*, 17 Feb. 2018, charlotteobserver.com. Accessed 19 May 2020.

4. Crossman, "A Daytona Legend."

5. Tom Gillispie. *Angel in Black: Remembering Dale Earnhardt Sr.* Cumberland House, 2008. 176.

Chapter 2. A Legacy of Racing

1. Leigh Montville. *At the Altar of Speed: The Fast Life and Tragic Death of Dale Earnhardt.* Doubleday, 2001. 20.

2. "The Total Novice's Guide to Dirt Track Racing." *Axle Addict*, 23 Jan. 2019, axleaddict.com. Accessed 19 May 2020.

3. Montville, *At the Altar of Speed*, 26.

4. "Plenty of Dad to be Found in Kerry Earnhardt." *HeraldNet*, 16 July 2004, heraldnet.com. Accessed 19 May 2020.

5. Montville, *At the Altar of Speed*, 38.

Chapter 3. Beginning His Career

1. Leigh Montville. *At the Altar of Speed: The Fast Life and Tragic Death of Dale Earnhardt.* Doubleday, 2001. 49.

2. Montville, *At the Altar of Speed*, 41.

3. "Dale Earnhardt." *Encyclopedia*, 27 Apr. 2020, encyclopedia.com. Accessed 19 May 2020.

4. Montville, *At the Altar of Speed*, 46.

5. Greg Fielden. "The Energy Shortage, Multiple Rules Changes—and Petty Wins 5th Title." *Stock Car Racing History*, 24 Nov. 2010, stockcarracinghistory.com. Accessed 19 May 2020.

Chapter 4. Rising Star of NASCAR

1. Leigh Montville. *At the Altar of Speed: The Fast Life and Tragic Death of Dale Earnhardt.* Doubleday, 2001. 68.

2. Montville, *At the Altar of Speed*, 65–66.

3. "Dale Earnhardt Sr.: Guts Make a Champ." *Famous Sports Stars*, n.d., sports.jrank.org. Accessed 19 May 2020.

Chapter 5. The Intimidator

1. David Poole. *Tim Richmond: The Fast Life and Remarkable Times of NASCAR's Top Gun*. Sports Publishing, 2013.

2. Leigh Montville. *At the Altar of Speed: The Fast Life and Tragic Death of Dale Earnhardt*. Doubleday, 2001. 143.

3. Robert G. Hagstrom. *The NASCAR Way: The Business that Drives the Sport*. Wiley, 2001. 143–144.

4. Hagstrom, *The NASCAR Way*, 143–144.

5. Joe Menzer. "Richard Childress Recalls the Gamble on Dale Earnhardt that Almost Broke Him." *Fox Sports*, 15 Nov. 2016, foxsports.com. Accessed 19 May 2020.

6. "NASCAR's Richard Childress Racing Finds On-Track Advantage in the Cloud." *Rescale*, n.d., resources.rescale.com. Accessed 19 May 2020.

7. Michelle R. Martinelli. "Dale Earnhardt Jr. on Why His Dad's Infamous 'Pass in the Grass' All-Star Race Was So Incredible." *USA Today*, 18 May 2017, ftw.usatoday.com. Accessed 19 May 2020.

8. "CUP: 'Junk Yard Dogs,' Childress Open Up about Earnhardt on Race Hub." *Fox News*, 11 Sept. 2015, foxnews.com. Accessed 19 May 2020.

9. Montville, *At the Altar of Speed*, 91.

10. Montville, *At the Altar of Speed*, 178.

Chapter 6. Rough Roads

1. Dakota Randall. "Check Out This Chilling Dale Earnhardt Sr. Death Threat Letter from 1987." *NESN*, 14 May 2018. nesn.com. Accessed 19 May 2020.

2. Shav Glick. "Stunning Finish at Daytona." *Los Angeles Times*, 19 Feb. 1990, latimes.com. Accessed 19 May 2020.

3. Leigh Montville. *At the Altar of Speed: The Fast Life and Tragic Death of Dale Earnhardt*. Doubleday, 2001. 140.

4. Montville, *At the Altar of Speed*, 139.

Continued

5. "Honoring 50 Greatest Drivers." *Motorsport*, 13 Feb. 1998, motorsport.com. Accessed 19 May 2020.

6. David Caraviello. "NASCAR CUP: Dislocated Sternum Couldn't Slow Dale Earnhardt in 1996." *Racing News*, 2 Mar. 2013, racingnews.co. Accessed 19 May 2020.

7. Caraviello, "NASCAR CUP."

8. "A Disoriented Dale Earnhardt Sr. at Darlington Raceway." *Racing News*, 6 Jan. 2018, racingnews.co. Accessed 19 May 2020.

Chapter 7. The Last Lap

1. Eric Adelson. "The Day Dale Earnhardt Died." *PostGame*, 13 Feb. 2011, thepostgame.com. Accessed 19 May 2020.

2. Adelson, "The Day Dale Earnhardt Died."

3. Adelson, "The Day Dale Earnhardt Died."

4. Austin Anderson. "How Long Is the Daytona 500? Number of Laps, Stages, Cars & More about the 'Great American Race.'" *Sporting News*, 17 Feb. 2020, sportingnews.com. Accessed 19 May 2020.

5. Eric Baxter. "How NASCAR Drafting Works: The Three Ds of NASCAR Racing." *How Stuff Works*, 5 Dec. 2008, howstuffworks.com. Accessed 19 May 2020.

6. Shav Glick. "Blame in Death of Earnhardt Shifts to Belt." *Los Angeles Times*, 24 Feb. 2001, latimes.com. Accessed 19 May 2020.

7. Adelson, "The Day Dale Earnhardt Died."

8. Don Coble. "Ten after 3: Sterling Marlin's Bump of Dale Earnhardt Changed Everything." *Jacksonville*, 7 Feb. 2011, jacksonville.com. Accessed 19 May 2020.

9. "'We've Lost Dale Earnhardt' Seven-Time Champion Dies in Daytona 500 Wreck." *Trentonian*, 19 Feb. 2001, trentonian.com. Accessed 19 May 2020.

10. Leigh Montville. *At the Altar of Speed: The Fast Life and Tragic Death of Dale Earnhardt*. Doubleday, 2001. 185–186.

Chapter 8. The Aftermath

1. David Newton. "Earnhardt Service Is Short and Solemn." *Daily Press*, 23 Feb. 2001, dailypress.com. Accessed 19 May 2020.

2. Newton, "Earnhardt Service Is Short and Solemn."

3. Newton, "Earnhardt Service Is Short and Solemn."

4. "Dale Earnhardt Jr., Ken Schrader Share Poignant Moment on 'Dale Jr. Download.'" *NASCAR*, 11 Mar. 2020, nascar.com. Accessed 19 May 2020.

5. Sandra McKee. "Answers from NASCAR Leave Open Questions." *Baltimore Sun*, 25 Feb. 2001, baltimoresun.com. Accessed 7 July 2020.

6. "Driver Marlin: Earnhardt Accident Wasn't My Fault." *ABC News*, 7 Jan. 2006, abcnews.go.com. Accessed 19 May 2020.

7. Karen Travers, Mark Flamini, and Jessica Small. "10 Years Later: How Dale Earnhardt's Death at Daytona 500 Changed NASCAR." *ABC News*, 18 Feb. 2011, abcnews.go.com. Accessed 19 May 2020.

8. Sara Lentati. "The Death that Changed NASCAR." *BBC*, 29 Apr. 2015, bbc.com. Accessed 19 May 2020.

Chapter 9. Remembering Dale Earnhardt Sr.

1. Leigh Montville. *At the Altar of Speed: The Fast Life and Tragic Death of Dale Earnhardt*. Doubleday, 2001. 131–132.

2. Montville, *At the Altar of Speed*, 131–132.

3. Steve Almasy. "Dale Earnhardt Jr. Is Among the Most Popular Drivers Ever. Here's a Look at His Career." *CNN*, 15 Aug. 2019, cnn.com. Accessed 19 May 2020.

4. "Dale Jr. Wins 2001 Pepsi 400 at Daytona." *NBC Sports*, n.d., nbcsports.com. Accessed 19 May 2020.

5. Michelle R. Martinelli. "Dale Jr. and Jeffrey Earnhardt Talk about the Pressure of the Family Legacy." *USA Today*, 5 Mar. 2019, ftw.usatoday.com. Accessed 19 May 2020.

6. Viv Bernstein. "Without Racing or Earnhardt, a Shop Remains." *New York Times*, 15 May 2009, nytimes.com. Accessed 19 May 2020.

7. "Kings Dominion Intimidator 305." *Kings Dominion*, n.d., kingsdominion.com. Accessed 19 May 2020.

8. "Intimidator: Gentlemen Start Your Engines!" *Carowinds*, n.d., carowinds.com. Accessed 19 May 2020.

9. "Dale Earnhardt's 76 NASCAR Cup Series Victories." *NASCAR*, 7 Apr. 2020, nascar.com. Accessed 19 May 2020.

10. "The Intimidator." *Bleacher Report*, n.d., bleacherreport.com. Accessed 19 May 2020.

Index

ABOUT THE AUTHOR

Marcia Amidon Lusted is the author of 175 books and more than 600 magazine articles for young readers. She is the former editor of *AppleSeeds* magazine and also works in sustainable development. She was once part of the crew for her husband's Sports Car Club of America (SCCA) amateur racing team.